My Food Explorer Book

A Playful Guide to Trying New Foods

Written by Victoria Milbrath, RD
and Kathryn Yao, M.Sc. OT

TABLE OF CONTENTS

INTRODUCTION

We know how hard it can be as parents to have a picky eater. Not only is it stressful not knowing if your child is meeting all their nutritional needs, but it also has a huge impact on your family's daily routine. Every activity in this book was made with the intention of empowering your child to feel comfortable exploring new foods, in the hopes of increasing their diet variety.

As registered dieticians and occupational therapists who work with many picky eaters, we know that repeated and positive exposure is key to introducing new foods. The science behind all our activities is food play. Food play is an evidence-based approach to help picky eaters explore new foods in a fun and positive way. We've used this approach with many different picky eaters over the past few years, and what a difference it made – not only did it boost the child's confidence and better their relationship with food, but it also positively impacted the family's overall wellbeing. We hope that through our activities, you will be able to achieve the same with your child and family!

There are several books tailored to parents, giving strategies on how to resolve picky eating. However, there is no activity book that is solely geared toward children, allowing them to be in control of their own feeding journey. Research has proven time and again that when children set their own goals, they are more likely to achieve them. This book includes different sections to explore different foods with your child. Before each section, please read the parental guide to understand how to best navigate each chapter. Bear in mind that these activities are only a skeleton and a guide - you can explore much more with your child. And most importantly, always follow your child's rhythm and comfort level.

DISCLAIMER

This book is not a guarantee that your child will be willing to eat more/new foods or resolve picky eating. This information is not intended as a substitute for professional medical advice, emergency treatment, or formal first-aid training.

Beware of foods that can be a choking hazard. If your child has a known allergy or intolerance, please be mindful of the foods that you present.

Change the activity based on your child's needs and abilities. We are giving general and evidence-based practice guidelines, but this might not apply to your child's specific needs. This book should ALWAYS be used under parental supervision.

Neither the authors shall be liable for any physical, psychological, emotional, financial, or commercial damages, including but not limited to special, incidental, consequential, or other damages. Our views and rights are the same: You (the legal guardians) are responsible for your and your child's own choices, actions, and results.

ACTIVITY 1

FOODS THAT HELP ME GROW

The first step to any change is to set a goal. It is known that if kids set their own goals, they are more motivated to go through the plan. This section goes through different concepts of food, setting a goal, and discussing responsibilities at mealtimes.

Here are some recommendations and tips to go through this section:

- Why is having a varied diet important? – This section is important to give purpose to eating a variety of foods. Why do I need to be strong? What's the point of having energy?

  Ask your child what they love to do. Do they love to play soccer? Play hockey? Play video games? Well, all these things require concentration, healthy muscles, and lots of energy. By eating food, we can feel good in our bodies while doing the things that we love.

- How do different foods give nutrients to different parts of the body?

  Although this might be generalized and extremely simplified, this gives children very concrete reasons to have a varied diet. You can go through all the different body parts and just have a sense of how a variety of foods will impact every part of the body.

PARENTAL GUIDE

- Being conscious of their own diet.

  This is a tricky part. Now that your child understands why it is important to eat different foods, let's find out if they have a varied diet. This activity will help them categorize each food that they like, and understand how it will help different body parts grow.

- Finding out if your child has a varied diet

  The most important thing is to notice any body parts that have a lot of foods (ex: more than three foods in a category) and any body parts that might have too little foods (ex: zero to two foods). Show your child how this body part might not have enough energy to grow strong and that we need to help the body part by adding a new food. This is when you set up the goal.

NOTE: We are aware that although there is data and clinical reasoning behind our statements, we have definitely generalized the information to cater to a child's level of understanding. Please take this information with a grain of salt, and you are encouraged to complete your own research!

WHY SHOULD I EAT DIFFERENT FOODS?

Eating different foods keep me healthy so I can:

Play

Learn at School

Read

Be Happy

Play with Pets

Play with Friends

Be Strong

FOODS THAT HELP BODY PARTS GROW

BRAIN
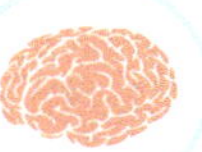
salmon,
broccoli,
nuts

EYES

yolk,
carrots,
sweet potato

LUNGS
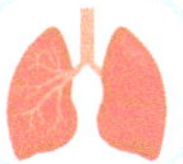
beets,
apples,
peppers

INTESTINES
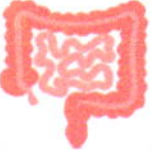
prunes,
yogurt,
cucumber

HAIR

avocado,
banana,
nuts

SKIN
salmon,
nuts,
cauliflower

HEART

tomatoes,
avocado,
blueberries

MUSCLES

meat,
eggs,
chickpeas

BONES

milk,
cheese,
broccoli

INSTRUCTIONS

1. Look through to pages 13-18. Look at all of the foods that help us grow and cut out the ones that you enjoy eating.

2. When you cut out all the foods you enjoy, turn to the back of each food to see which body parts they help grow.

3. Go to pages 9-11 and place the food onto the right body part. If you have a food that has multiple body parts, you can choose which one you want to add it to.

Optional: If there are more foods that you like, draw them on the empty squares. Just make sure to look up what the food is good for and place it in the right category!

Psst! If you want to redo this activity, go on abcyum.ca/collections/book-collection to have a printable version.

FOODS THAT HELP BODY PARTS GROW

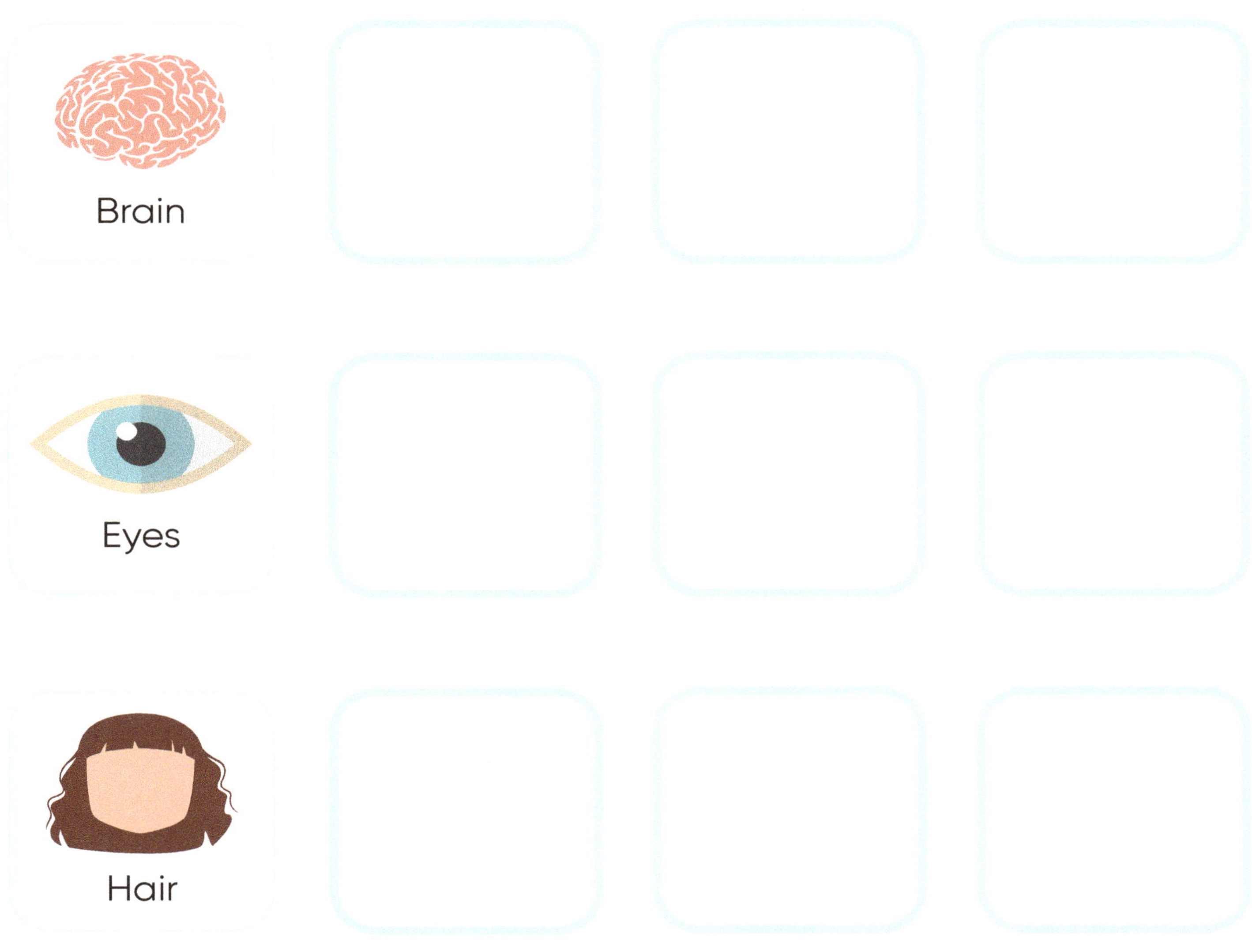

FOODS THAT HELP BODY PARTS GROW

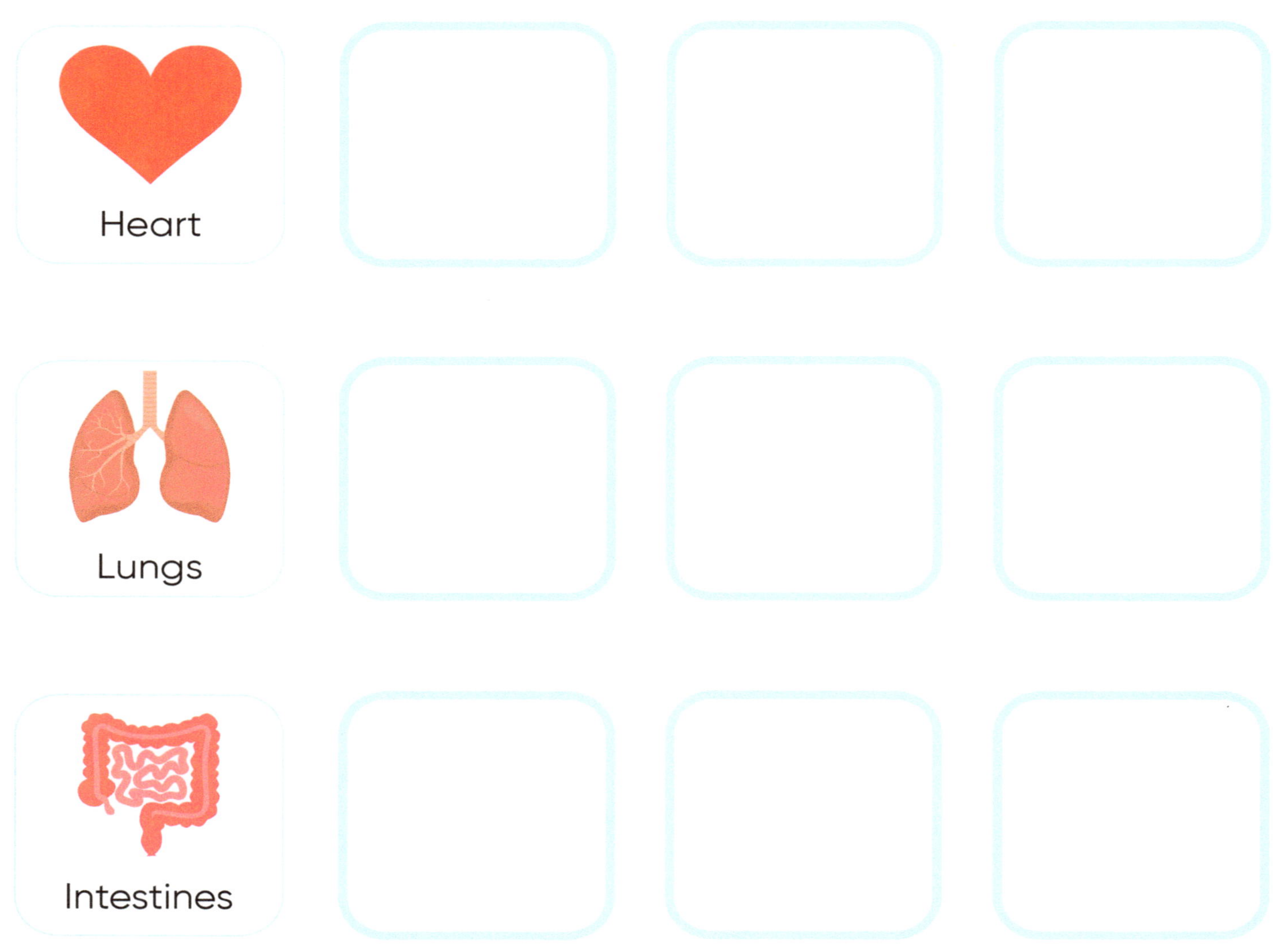

FOODS THAT HELP BODY PARTS GROW

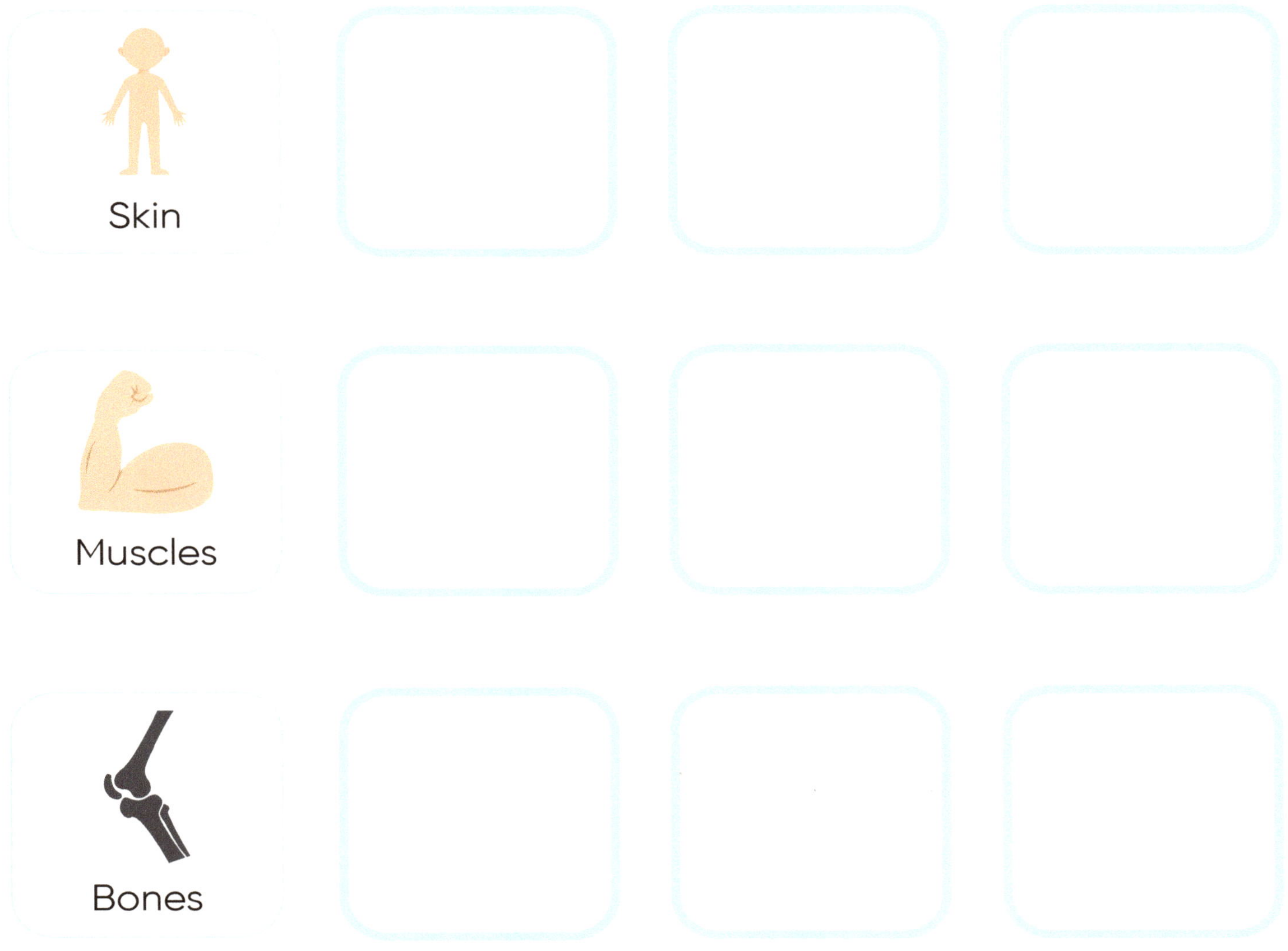

FOODS

 Hotdog

 Burger

 Apple

 Banana

 Milk

 Egg

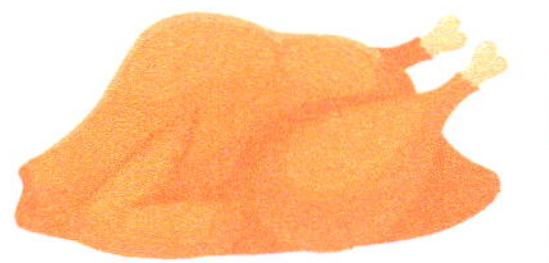 Chicken

 Broccoli

 Peas

 Tomato

 Carrot

 Corn

 Cucumber

 Porridge

 Raspberries

 Taco

FOODS

FOODS

 Strawberries

 Applesauce

 Grapes

 Chicken Nuggets

 Potatoes

 Cheese

 Blueberries

 Pizza

 Ice Cream

 Spaghetti

 Rice

 Bread

 Salmon

 Celery

 Salad

 Pancakes

FOODS

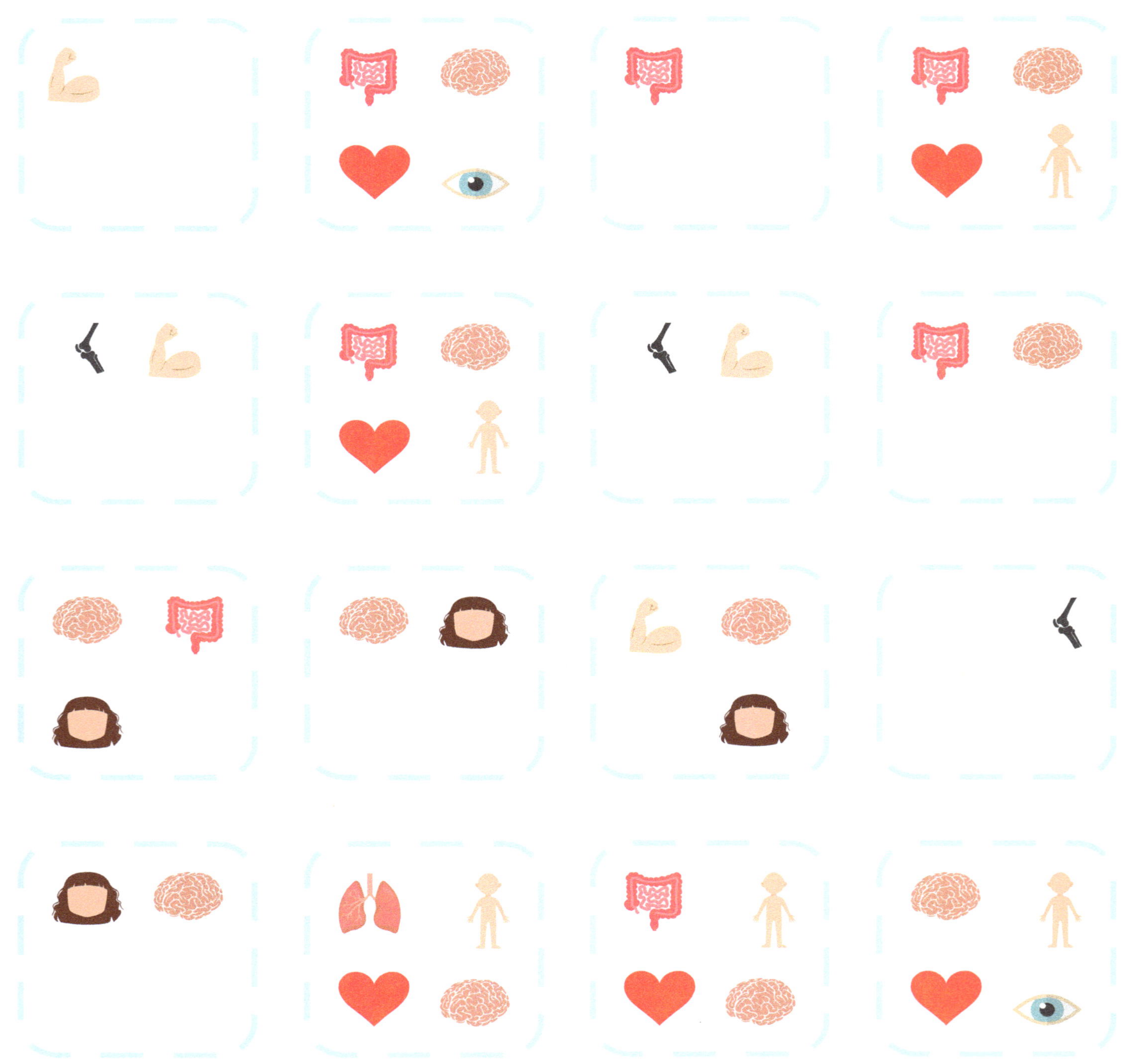

FOODS

 Watermelon

 Sandwich

 Peanut Butter

Beans

 Pineapple

 Yogurt

 Avocado

 Nuts

 Beets

 Bell Pepper

 Orange

 Steak

 Cereal

 Crackers

Draw your own food

Draw your own food

FOODS

look up what this food
is good for
look up what this food
is good for

MY EATING GOAL

Out of the foods that you classified on pages 9–11, circle the body parts that have two foods or less.

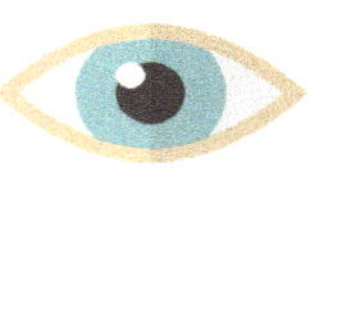 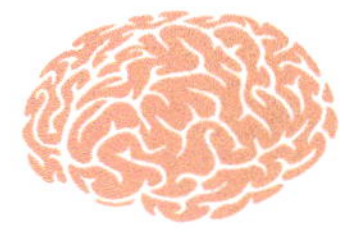 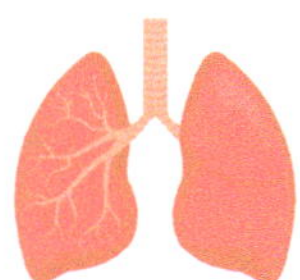  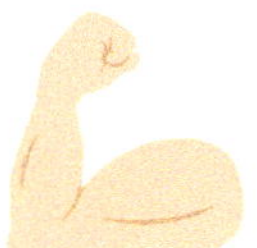

   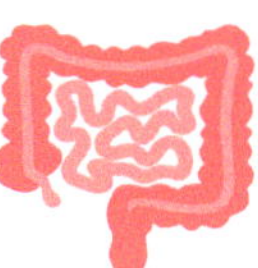

These are the body parts that might not have enough nutrients to grow strong.

Let's pick one body part that you will help grow strong and healthy.

I want to help my ________________.

body part

MY EATING GOAL

To help my ________________ , I need to set up a GOAL

body part

to eat something new.

My goal is to:

(circle the action you want to do)

lick

chew and spit

chew and swallow

____

write a food that you would like to try

so that I can grow strong and healthy.

Remember: you will <u>NEVER</u> be forced to eat

something you are not ready for.

RESPONSIBILITY CONTRACT

My parents' responsibilities
and
My responsibilities

PARENTAL GUIDE

Did you know that both parents and children have their own respective responsibilities during mealtime? This section outlines your responsibilities, as parents, as well as your child's responsibilities. This is called the Division of Responsibility, coined by Ellyn Satter. It is based on the premise that with a proper positive environment and the right support, mealtimes are a lot more positive and stress-free.

What is the Division of Responsibility? In short:

Parents are responsible for determining:
- What meal will be served
- When and where the family will eat

Children are responsible for determining:
- How much food they will eat
- Which foods they choose to eat (out of the foods that you have presented)

PARENTAL GUIDE

Let's get started with these different tips

1)   Empower your child by giving control (and sharing the responsibility!)

     It's important to understand that you can only control so much during mealtimes. The more pressure you put on your child, the more your child might resist and associate negative feelings with mealtimes. Remember your responsibilities, and when you feel the anxiety and stress bubble up, remember to breathe and try your hardest to stay cool.

2)   Maintain a routine and be consistent.

     The division of responsibility takes time to implement and obtain the desired results. It might take a few days to a few weeks before your child starts trying new foods and eating more on their plate.

3)   Serve preferred and non-preferred foods together during a meal.

     For example, if you want to introduce broccoli, and your child really enjoys chicken nuggets, put chicken nuggets on the table along with the broccoli.

This will decrease both your anxiety and your child's anxiety, as you both know that there is a food available at mealtimes that they enjoy eating. However, keep pairing new foods with this preferred food! Do not expect them to eat the broccoli – just the exposure to the new food (ex: tolerating broccoli on the plate or playing with the broccoli) will get your child more comfortable with the new food. Did you know that it takes up to 20 exposures before a food is NOT considered new?

4)   Go through the following pages with your child.

This will help your child concretely understand their own responsibilities and your responsibilities. Once you and your child understand your own responsibilities, read the contract. Sign the contract as a commitment that both parties will respect their own responsibilities.

MY PARENTS' RESPONSIBILITIES

Check off the boxes, as you and your parents complete your responsibilities!

- ☐ Choose what meal will be served. Don't worry, they will make sure that there will always be at least one food that you like
- ☐ Present to you balanced meals and snacks to make sure you grow
- ☐ Choose where meals and snacks will be eaten
- ☐ Choose when meals and snacks will be eaten
- ☐ Teach you appropriate behaviors at the table
- ☐ Be a good role model
- ☐ Try out new foods together

MY RESPONSIBILITIES

Check off the boxes, as you and your parents complete your responsibilities!

- ☐ I choose how much food I need to eat until I feel good
- ☐ I choose which foods I want to eat out of the options offered on the table
- ☐ I need to learn and show expected behaviors (manners) at the table
- ☐ I can try new foods at the table with my parents

THE MEAL CONTRACT

For the Parents:

I understand and agree to my responsibilities listed above during the meal contract. I will follow through on all of my responsibilities.

For the Child:

I understand and agree to my responsibilities.
I understand the consequences to my actions.
I have the power to choose how much and whether I want to eat the food that is provided. If I choose not to finish, I am telling my mom and my dad that I am not hungry and that is okay. I get a choice of 1 snack after the meal. If I am hungry, I will have to wait for my next meal to eat.

________________________   ________________________

child's signature   parent's signature

ACTIVITY 2

EXPLORING FOOD THROUGH SENSES

INSTRUCTIONS

This activity will help with sensory exploration with foods. This will simply allow you to learn about new foods and become more comfortable with them. You will also be able to describe the food and tell your parents exactly what you don't like or like about it. Is it the smell? Is it the taste? Is it too tough? Does the crunch make too much noise?

Let's explore!

Psst! If you want to redo this activity, go on abcyum.ca/collections/book-collection to have a printable version.

Instructions:

1. Choose a food of your choice that you want to explore with all of your senses. Start with a food that you enjoy eating. To challenge yourself, choose a food you don't really like.

2. Flip to page 32 to start exploring the food through all of your senses! Read all of the questions on the left page. You can answer the questions by saying the answer out loud.
There is not always a right or wrong answer. Everyone has a different sensory experience with different foods.

3. Once you go through all of the senses, turn to page 46 to summarize the food! You can hang up the "description of food" page on your fridge or even in your room!

WHAT ARE OUR SENSES?

Humans have five basic senses:

touch, sight, hearing, smell and taste

  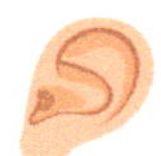  

These senses give us information about our world and helps us understand what is going around us.

Did you know that we use all of these 5 senses when eating?

Let's explore!

THE 5 SENSES

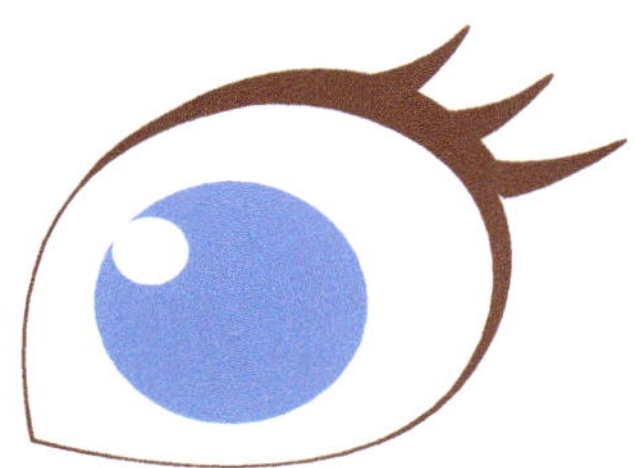

Sight:
This let's us see
what's around us.

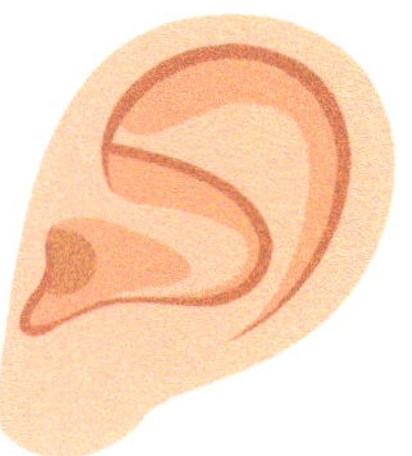

Hearing:
This let's us hear
sounds around us.

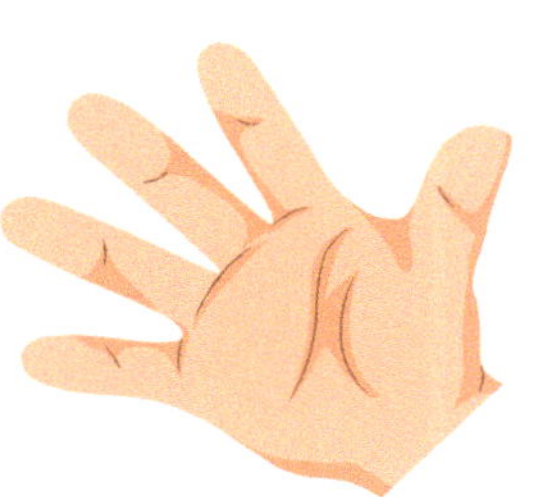

Touch:
This let's us feel
objects around us.

Smell:
This let's us smell
the aromas
around us.

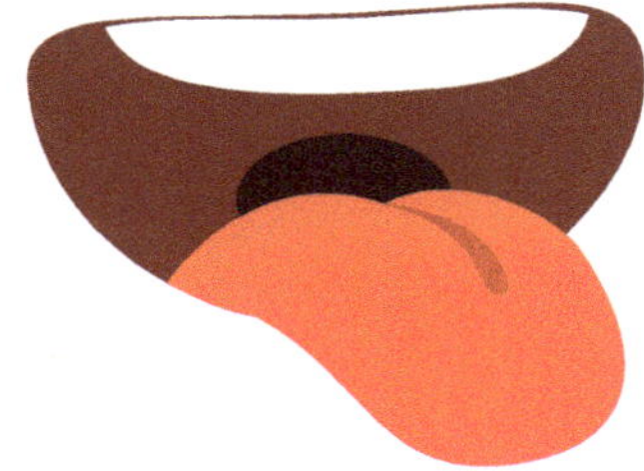

Taste:
This let's us taste
food.

SIGH

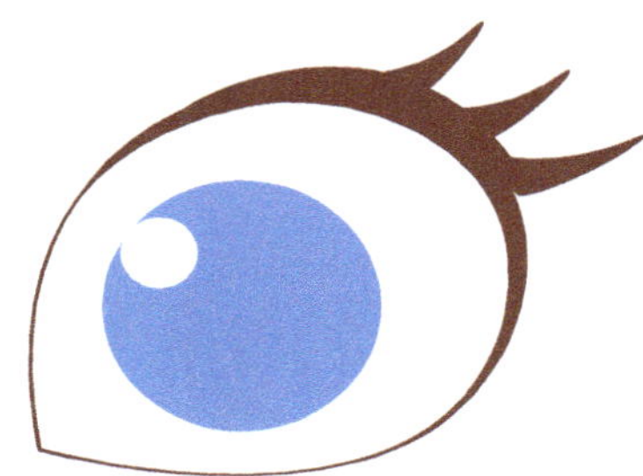

Look at the food. What do you see? Without touching it, describe the food in front of you.

- What shape is it?

- What color is it?

- Is it flat or tall?

- Is it bumpy or smooth?

- Is it big or small?

- When you cut into the food, does it look the same or different from the outside?

SIGHT

SHAPES

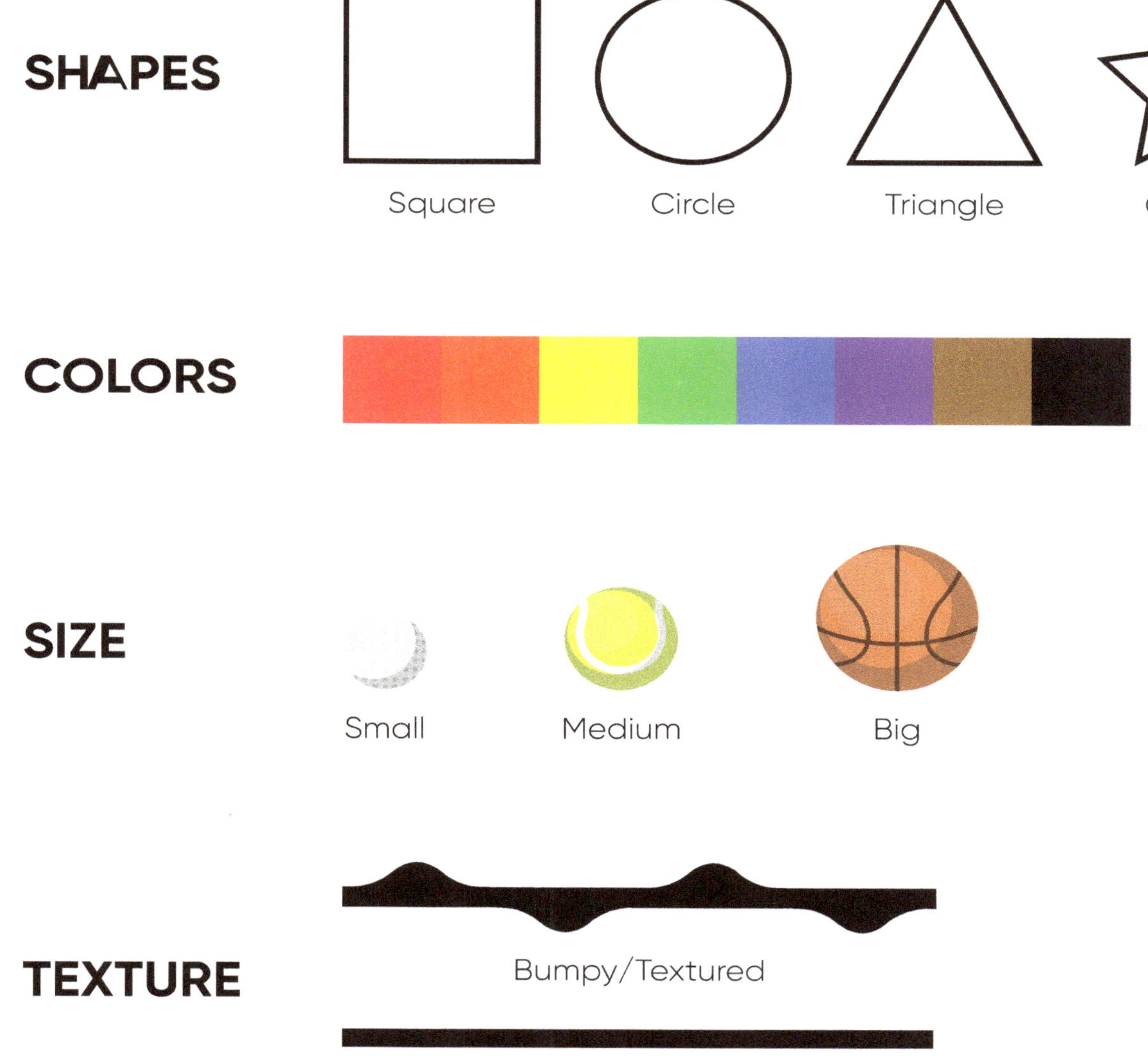

COLORS

SIZE

TEXTURE

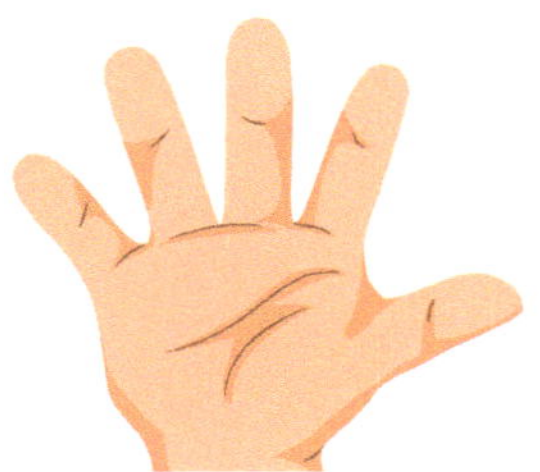

Touch and play with the food. How does the food feel in your hands? Describe the food in front of you.

- Is it soft or hard? Is it mushy, wet, or dry?

- Is it grainy, bumpy, or smooth?

- Is it squishy, soft, liquid, hard, or bubbly?

- Is it sticky or oily?

- Is it room temperature, hot, or cold?

- Is it light or heavy?

TOUCH - 1

TEXTURE

Bumpy

Smooth

Dry

Sticky

Liquid

Different textures

Slimy

TEMPERATURE

Cold

Room Temperature

Hot

WEIGHT

Light

Heavy

SOUND - 1

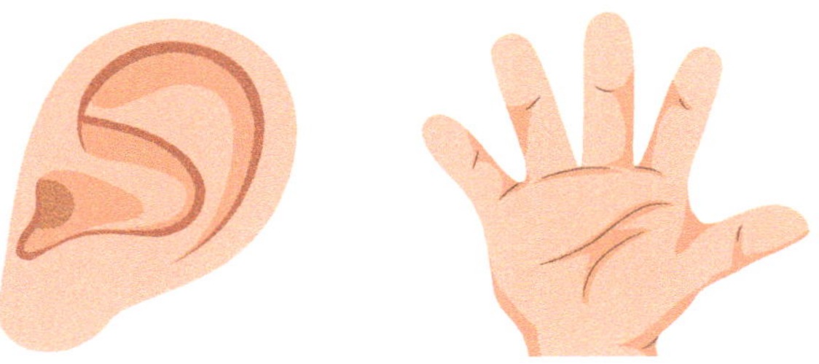

Let's play with the food in your hands. Squish it or roll it between your hands. What do you hear? Let's describe the food in front of you.

- Does it have a sound?

- Is the sound soft or loud?

- Is the sound squeaky or crunchy?

- Do you hear popping and fizzing?

SOUND - 1

INTENSITY

No Sound

Quiet

Loud

TYPES OF NOISE

Crunchy

Liquid

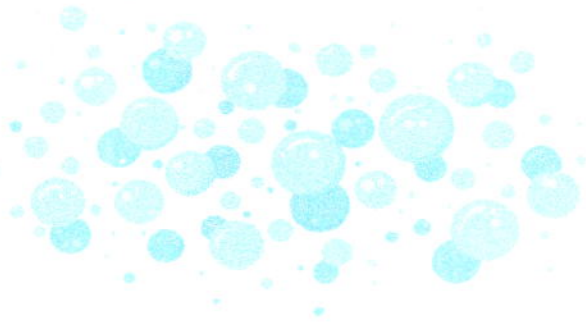

Fizz

Squeaky

SMELL

Bring the food close to your nose. What do you smell? Describe the food in front of you.

- Does it have a smell?

- Is the smell faint or strong?

- Does it smell sweet, sour, or salty?

- Does it smell fruity, savory, or flowerly?

- Does it smell like something you already know (ex. chocolate, cake)?

SMELL

INTENSITY

0%	10%	50%	100%
No Smell	Dull	Medium	Strong

Sweet  Salty  Sour

TYPES OF SMELL

Fruity  Savory  Flowery

Spicy  Bitter

TOUCH - 2

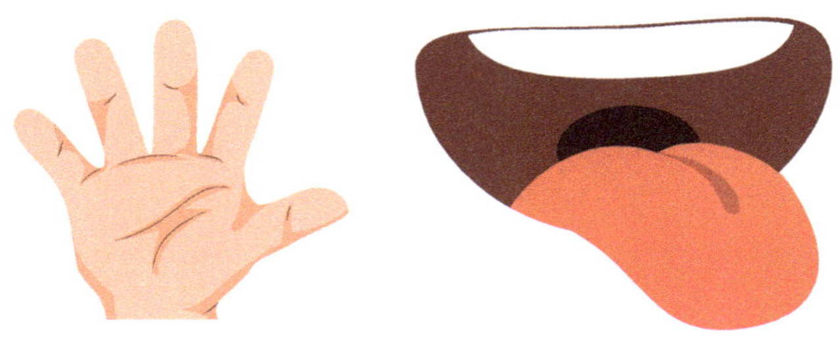

If you are ready, put the food in your mouth. How does it feel? Describe the food in your mouth.

- Is it soft or hard? Is it mushy, wet, or dry?

- Is it grainy, bumpy, or smooth?

- Is it squishy, soft, liquid, hard? Is it bubbly?

- Is it sticky or oily?

- Is it room temperature, hot, or cold?

- Is it light or heavy?

TOUCH - 2

TEXTURE

Bumpy

Smooth

Dry

Sticky

Liquid

Different textures

Slimy

TEMPERATURE

Cold

Room Temperature

Hot

WEIGHT

Light

Heavy

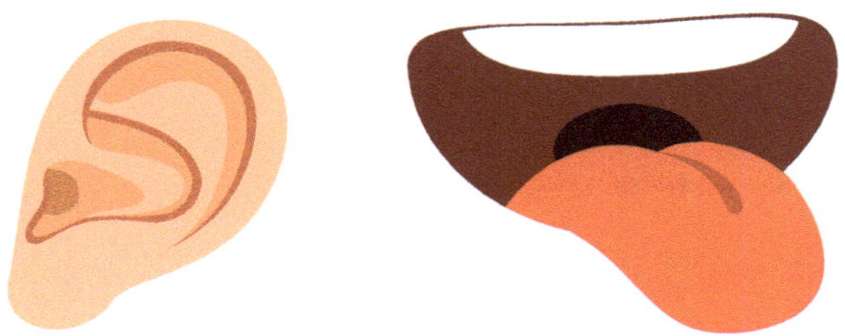

If you are ready, put the food in your mouth. Crunch the food. What does it sound like? Describe the food in your mouth.

- Does it have a sound?

- What does it sound like in **your** mouth?

- Is the sound squeaky or crunchy?

- Does it sound wet or dry?

- Does it fizz in your mouth?

SOUND - 2

INTENSITY

No Sound

Quiet

Loud

TYPES OF NOISE

Crunchy

Liquid

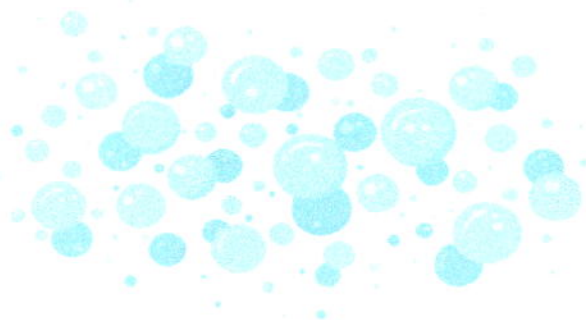

Fizz

Squeaky

TASTE

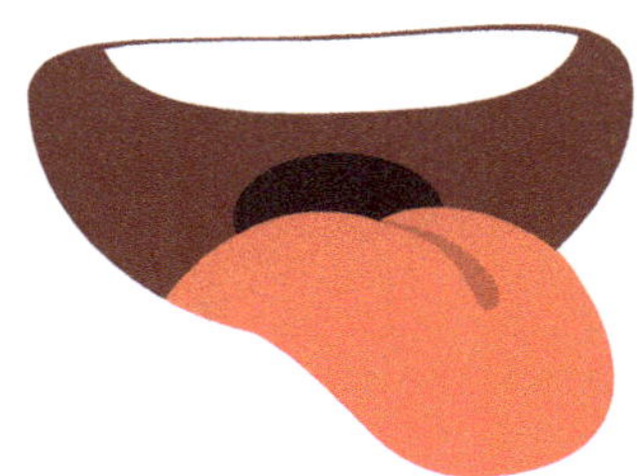

If you are ready, put the food in your mouth. How does it taste? Describe the food in your mouth.

- Is it sweet, salty, sour, or bitter?

- Is the taste mild or strong?

- Is it bland or does it have a lot of taste?

- Is it fruity, meaty, or nutty?

TASTE

INTENSITY

0%	10%	50%	100%
No Taste	Light	Medium	Strong

TYPES OF TASTE

Sweet — Salty — Sour — Bitter

Fruity — Meaty — Nutty

DESCRIPTION OF FOOD

Write or draw your answers for a food of your choice

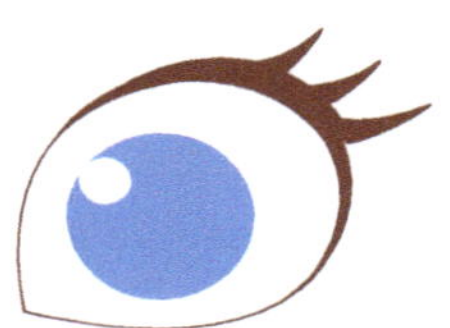

______ SHAPE   ______ COLOR   ______ SIZE   ______ TEXTURE

______ INTENSITY OF SMELL   ______ TYPE OF SMELL

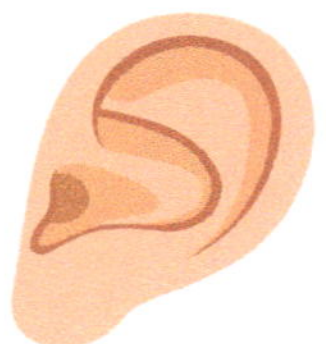

______ INTENSITY OF NOISE   ______ TYPE OF NOISE   ______ INTENSITY OF NOISE   ______ TYPE OF NOISE

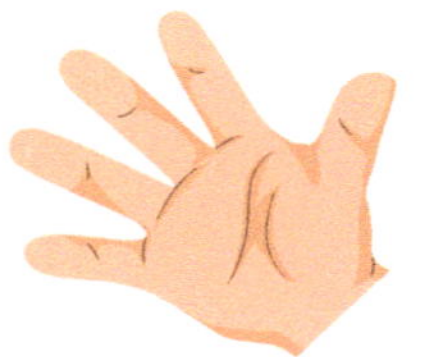

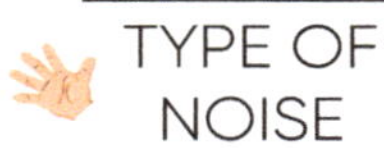 ______ TEXTURE    ______ TEXTURE   ______ TEMPERATURE   ______ WEIGHT

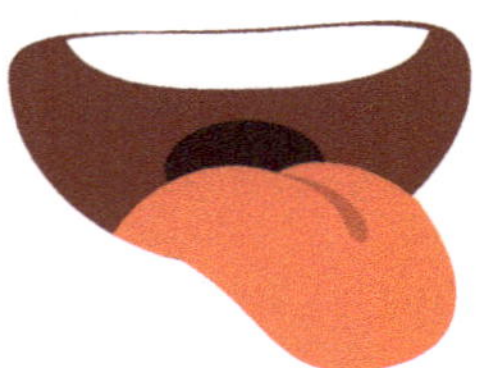

______ INTENSITY OF TASTE   ______ TYPES OF TASTE

ACTIVITY 3

WARM-UP BEFORE EATING

INSTRUCTIONS

DID YOU KNOW?

Did you know that eating takes more than 30 muscles to act in a coordinated fashion, in order to properly chew and swallow our food?!

WHY DO A WARM-UP BEFORE EATING?

We need to make sure that all of the muscles in our mouths are awake, so that we can chew and eat properly.

Let's try some of the exercises below to strengthen and workout the muscles of your mouth, tongue, and lips!

Have fun!

TONGUE

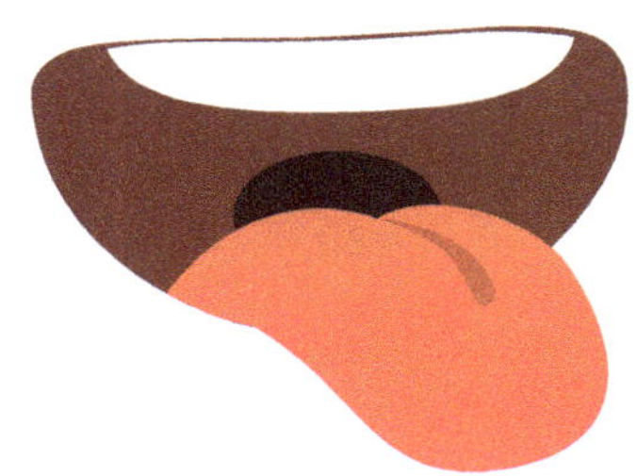

- Make your cheeks pop out by pressing your tongue to the side of your mouth

- Count your teeth with your tongue

- Lick your lips (you can put melted chocolates or jelly on your lips)

- Sing a song by saying "la, la, la"

- Try to touch your nose with your tongue

MOUTH

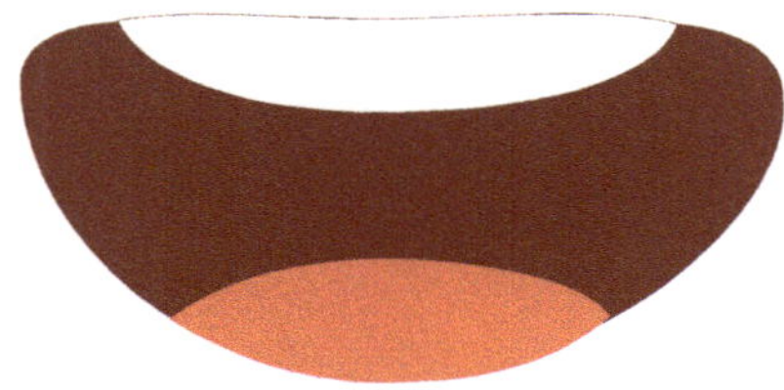

- Blow air kisses

- Blow through an empty straw

- Drink a liquid through a straw. You can make it harder by sucking up thicker substances (ex. yogurt or smoothie).

LIPS

- Make silly faces with your mouth

  ○ Make fish lips

  ○ Make an "O"

  ○ Make the biggest smile

  ○ Fill up your cheeks with air while keeping your lips closed (like a blow fish)

ACTIVITY 4

NUTRITION GAME

FIBER

WHAT IS FIBER?

Fiber is a very important nutrient found in plants (fruits and vegetables, grains, legumes, nuts and seeds). Fiber is important to help your body digest all the food you eat, it helps you go to the bathroom, and it helps you grow strong and healthy.

DID YOU KNOW?

Did you know that you need to eat 25 grams of fiber every day to stay healthy?

Did you know that most kids only eat between 5 and 15 grams per day?

DO YOU EAT ENOUGH FIBER?

Let's play a game to help you find out if you eat enough fiber! In this game, <u>1 point = 1 gram of fiber.</u>

NOTE: The amount of fiber for each food is generalized and might not always be accurate. If you want to be as precise as possible, you can change the number of points according to the amount of fiber in the food consumed.

INSTRUCTIONS

1. Turn to page 59. Look at all of the foods and cut out the ones that you enjoy eating.

2. Then, turn to pages 55-56 and place each food where you would like to eat it: at breakfast, as a snack, for lunch or supper.

3. Add up your points for each meal and snack of the day individually. Then, add all your points together (breakfast + snack + lunch + snack + supper). Write your total on page 56.

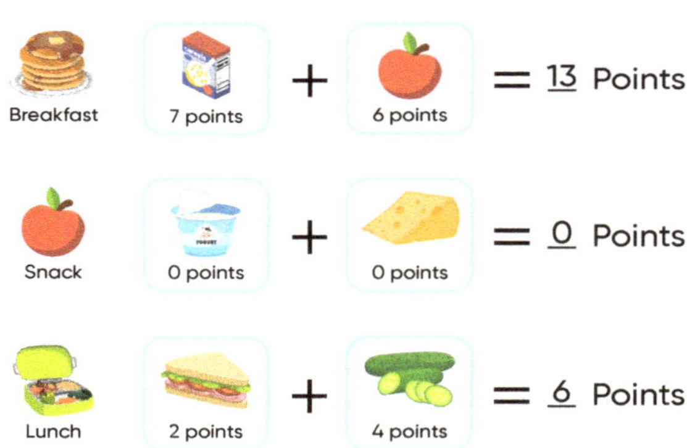

Psst! If you want to redo this activity, go on abcyum.ca/collections/book-collection to have a printable version.

FIBER

Breakfast

$+$ $=$ __ Points

Snack

$+$ $=$ __ Points

Lunch

$+$ $=$ __ Points

FIBER

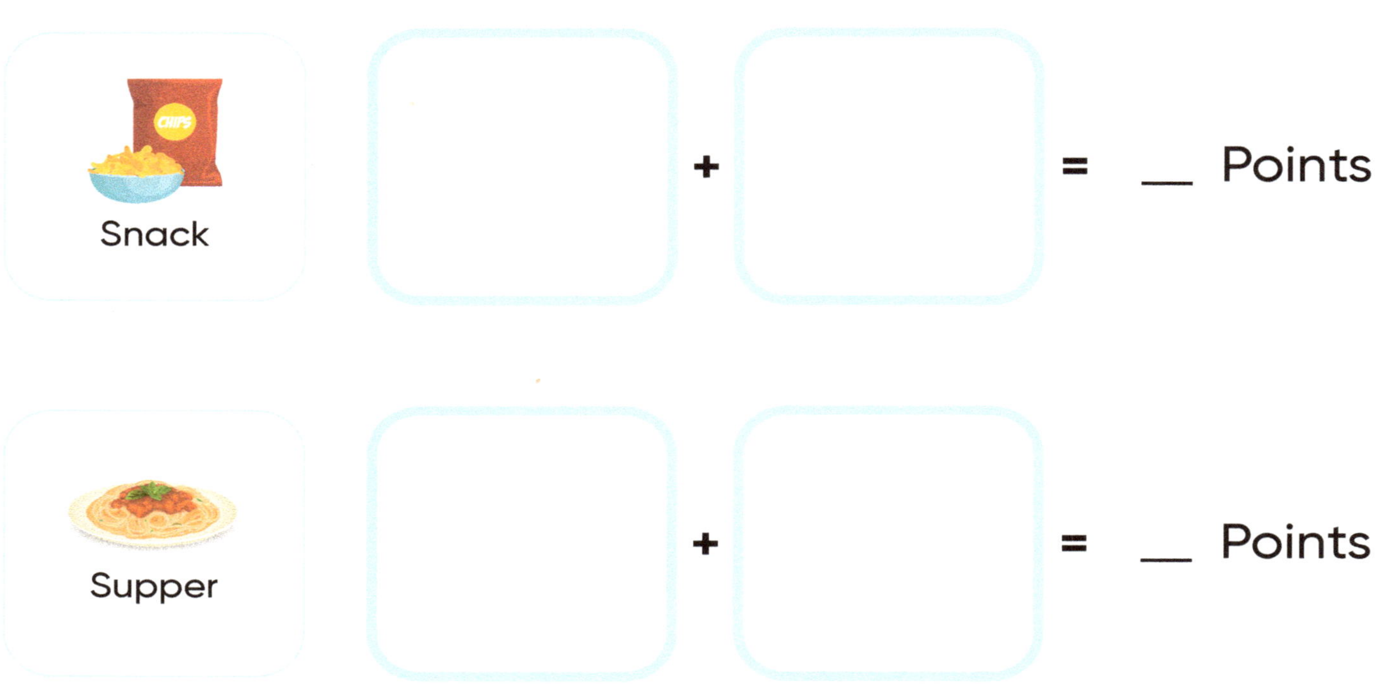

Snack   □ + □ = __ Points

Supper   □ + □ = __ Points

Now, add up all your points.
Remember: 1 point = 1 gram of fiber

TOTAL = ___g of fiber per day

FIBER

Do you have 25 points?

Circle your answer

YES   **No**

If you circled **YES,** congratulations! You eat enough fiber, keep it up.

If you circled **NO**, let's go back and add some foods you'd like to add to your diet to be as close to 25 points as possible.

This will keep you healthy and strong to play and do things that you like!

FRUITS

Watermelon
4 points

Orange
3 points

Pear
5 points

Apple
4 points

x10

Blueberries
2 points

x10

Raspberries
2 points

Banana
3 points

Grapes
3 points

Strawberry
4 points

Kiwi
5 points

X10

Blackberries
3 points

Pineapple
2 points

Mango
3 points

Cherries
3 points

Peach
4 points

Avacado
6 points

VEGETABLES

Peas
4 points

Corn
4 points

Carrot
4 points

Lettuce
4 points

Potatoes
2 points

Sweet Potato
4 points

Cucumber
4 points

Radish
4 points

Bell Pepper
4 points

Broccoli
4 points

Tomato
3 points

Celery
4 points

Cauliflower
4 points

Spinach
4 points

Asparagus
4 points

Beets
4 points

GRAINS

Crackers
4 points

Brown Bread
6 points

Bread
2 points

Porridge
6 points

Cereal
7 points

Cupcake
3 points

Pasta
3 points

Rice
3 points

Pancakes
1 point

Donuts
4 points

Waffles
2 points

Pizza
1 point

Burger
2 points

Sandwich
4 points

Chips
1 point

Popcorn
3 points

LEGUMES +
NUTS AND SEEDS

White Beans
7 points

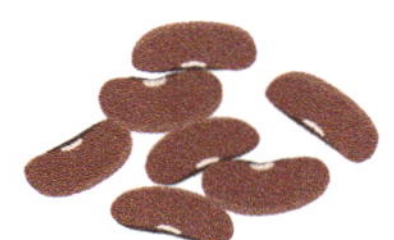

Kidney Beans
7 points

Black Beans
7 points

Chickpeas
5 points

Cashew
6 points

Peanuts
4 points

Almonds
4 points

Hazelnuts
4 points

Walnuts
4 point

Sunflower Seeds
4 points

Chia Seeds
7 points

Flaxseeds
7 point

DAIRY + MEATS

Milk
0 points

Cheese
0 points

Yogurt
0 points

Ice Cream
0 points

Egg
0 points

Chicken
0 points

Salmon
0 points

Steak
0 points

NOTE: Dairy and meats are 0 points because they do not have any fiber. They are still very important foods as they are a great source of protein, and have many other nutrients.

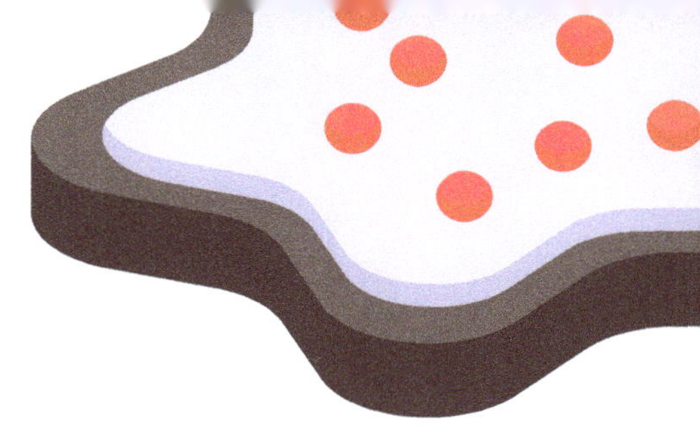

ACTIVITY 5

FOOD EXPERIMENTS

For Parents:
Everyone learns about new foods through repeated exposure, and sensory exploration. These food play ideas will allow your child to be exposed to foods multiple times and explore the food through all the senses, all while having fun! It's important not to pressure your child to eat/try the foods during sensory play. Just model your own enjoyment of the foods and have fun learning about new foods. The tasting part will come with time, practice, and patience. Enjoy!!

EXPERIMENT # 1

MAGIC WAND

Description of activity:
This activity will show you how to use 3 different foods to make a magic wand!

INSTRUCTIONS

Goal: The goal of this experiment is to explore new foods through play.

Materials needed:

- ☐ 3 fruits or 3 vegetables of different sizes (1 big, 1 medium and 1 small)

- ☐ Cookie cutters, scissors or child-safe knife

- ☐ Skewers

- ☐ Optional: melted chocolate if you use fruits

Preparation:

After you choose 3 fruits OR 3 vegetables, ask your parents to cut them into approximately 0.5 inch (1.5 cm) slices. Try to get the biggest surface area (for example: cut a slice in the middle of an kiwi rather than the edge). Make sure to remove peels that cannot be ingested.

INSTRUCTIONS

How to choose your foods

1) Choose your level of difficulty:

  • Level 1: Choose 3 foods that you enjoy eating
  • Level 2: Choose 1 foods that you enjoy eating and 2 foods
    that you do not enjoy eating yet
  • Level 3: Choose 3 foods that you do not enjoy eating yet

2) Choose your taste profile.
   Here are some examples of different sweet and savory
   combinations:

  • Sweet:
    Watermelon (big) apple (medium) banana (small)
    Kiwi (big) strawberry (medium) blueberry (small)
    Pinapple (big) orange (medium) raspberry (small)

  • Savoury:
    Bell pepper (big) cucumber (medium) cherry tomato (small)
    Lettuce (big) tomato (medium) cauliflower (small)
    Beets (big) radish (medium) mushroom (small)

MAGIC WAND ACTIVITY

Step #1:
Use a cookie cutter, a child-safe knife or scissors to cut the biggest fruit or vegetable into a star, the second biggest into a circle, and do what you want with the smallest one.

MAGIC WAND ACTIVITY

Step #2:
Let's start assembling the magic wand! Take the skewer and place the smallest food first. Then the circle. Lastly, place the star on top to finish off the wand.

MAGIC WAND ACTIVITY

Optional:
Dip the magic wand into a potion (ex. melted chocolate) and take a bite!

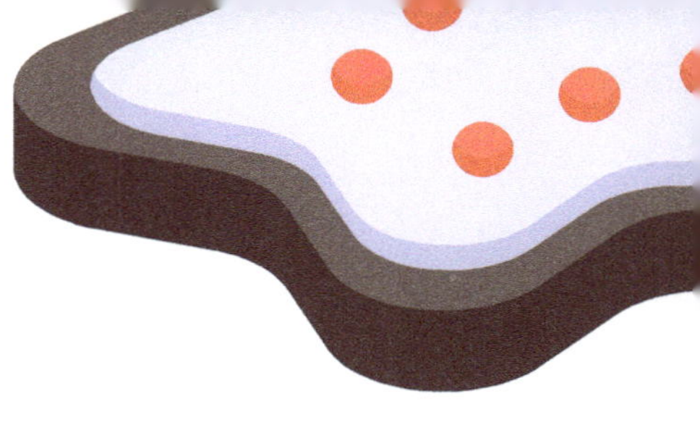

EXPERIMENT # 2
CUTTING

Description of activity:

Can you cut the foods into different shapes?

INSTRUCTIONS

Goal: The goal of this experiment is to explore new foods through play. As a bonus, this activity also works on copying and building skills.

Materials needed:

☐   Any food that keeps its form when cut

☐   Scissors or child-safe knife

Optional:

Place a piece of wax paper or parchment paper over the following pages to waterproof them.

Preparation:

Cut the food into approximately 0.5 inch (1.2 cm) slices. Try to get the biggest surface area (for example: cut a slice in the middle of an orange rather than the edge).

INSTRUCTIONS

How to choose your foods

1) Choose your level of difficulty:

- Level 1: Choose 3 foods that you enjoy eating
- Level 2: Choose 1 foods that you enjoy eating and 2 foods that you do not enjoy eating yet
- Level 3: Choose 3 foods that you do not enjoy eating yet

2) Choose your taste profile.
   Here are some examples of different sweet and savory foods:

- Sweet:
  Watermelon, apple, kiwi, orange, melon, pear, grapefruit

- Savoury:
  Bell pepper, cucumber, lettuce, tomato, beets, raddish, ham, salami, chicken, bacon, steak, pita, bread

CUTTING ACTIVITY

Using scissors, can you cut the food(s) that you chose into these shapes? You can place them on this page (if waterproofed), or on a plate.

CUTTING ACTIVITY

Using scissors, can you cut the food(s) that you chose into a t-shirt? Decorate the front with other foods!

Using scissors, can you cut the food(s) that you chose into a cape? Decorate your own superhero cape with food!

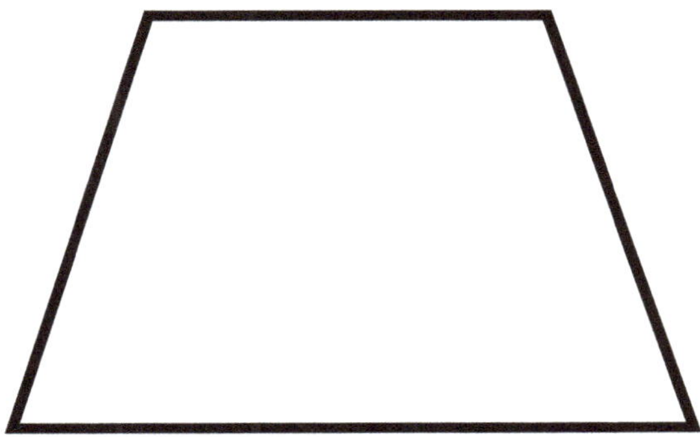

CUTTING ACTIVITY

Using a child-safe knife, can you cut the food(s) that you chose into a flower?

Using a child-safe knife, can you cut the food(s) that you chose into a robot? Decolate it however you like!

CUTTING ACTIVITY

By nibbling with your teeth, can you shape the food(s) that you chose into a house? If you don't like the food yet, you can spit it into a bowl.

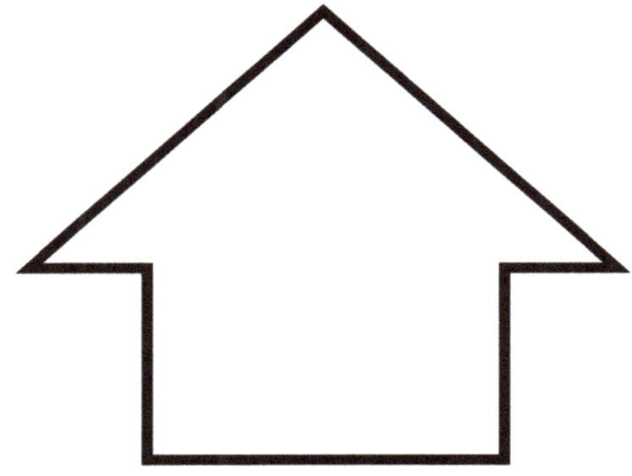

By nibbling with your teeth, can you shape the food(s) that you chose into a rocket? If you don't like the food yet, you can spit it into a bowl.

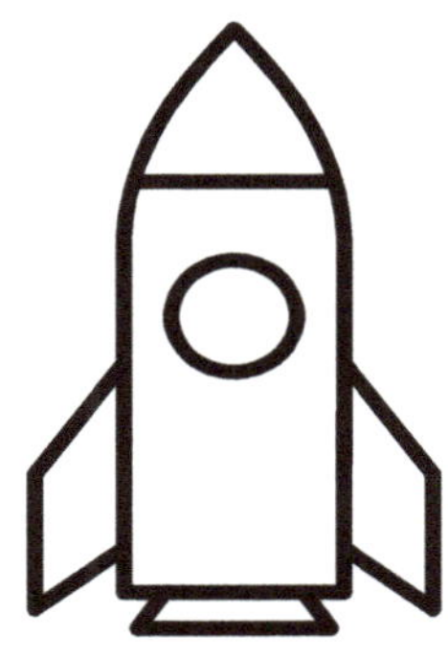

EXPERIMENT # 3

EDIBLE SENSORY BINS

Description of activity:
A sensory bin is typically a large container filled with different materials carefully selected to stimulate the senses. Young children learn best when they can touch and feel something. In this book, we want to present you 3 different **edible** sensory bins to help with food exploration!

SENSORY BIN ACTIVITY

Challenge #1 (SWEET SENSORY BIN)

1.   Crush some cereal to make sand-like texture OR add brown sugar into a clear bin.

2.   Add in some sliced fruits such as apples, bananas, oranges, etc

3.   Add some fun kitchen tools such as spoons, measuring cups, measuring spoons, etc.

Challenge #2 (SAVORY SENSORY BIN)

1.   Crush some crackers to make a sand-like texture. Add it into a clear bin.

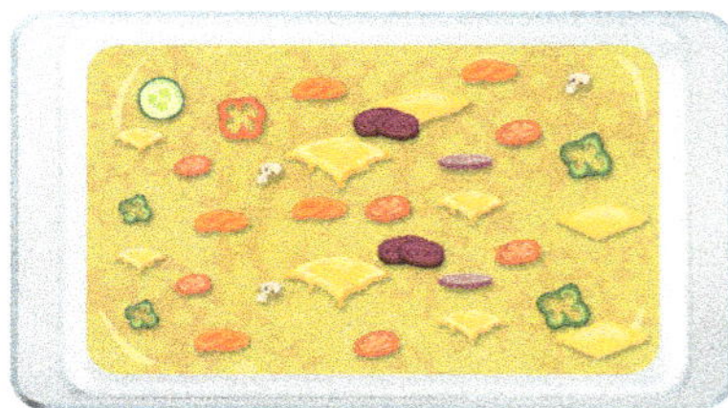

2.   Add in some cheese or vegetables to go in the crackers. You can cut the cheese and vegetables into different shapes!

3.   Add some fun kitchen tools such as spoons, measuring cups, measuring spoons, etc.

Challenge #3 (GUEWY SENSORY BIN)

1.   You can make an edible, guewy sensory bin using Jello and fruits. Make the Jello (as per the instructions on the Jello packet) and pour it into a clear bin or clear baking dish.

2.   Add a few berries into sensory bin.

3.   Let it rest in the fridge until settles and solidifies. Once it is ready, take it out and ask your kiddo to dig out the different fruits from the Jello! They can use a spoon, a fork, their hands, or even their mouths!

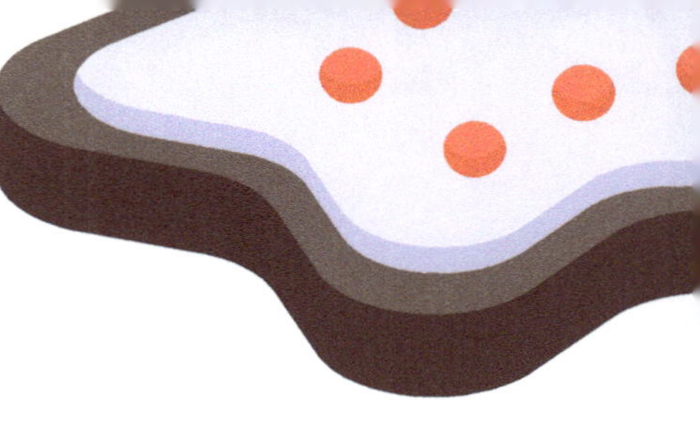

EXPERIMENT # 4

WHIPPED DRAWING

Description of activity:
This messy activity allows your child to draw shapes, numbers, or anything in their imagination in whipped cream! You can even add food coloring to change the colors.

INSTRUCTIONS

Goal: The goal of this experiment is to get your hands dirty and enjoy a creamy desert. You'll be stepping up your copying skills, drawing skills, and even handwriting skills!

Materials needed:

☐   Whipped cream

☐   Apron

☐   A big plate or cutting board

☐   Fruits

Optional: graham crackers, sprinkles, and/or utensils, food coloring – if you use food coloring, you will need bowls

Preparation:

1.   Since this activity is messy, make sure to protect your table or your work surface before starting (ex. using a tablecloth). If you decide to use food coloring, this might stain furniture or your tabletop.

INSTRUCTIONS

2.   Have towels nearby in case you want to wipe your hands. This will prevent a bigger mess. You can also wipe your hands on an apron or on an old t-shirt.

How to choose your foods

1) Choose your level of difficulty:

- Level 1: Choose 3 foods that you enjoy eating
- Level 2: Choose 1 foods that you enjoy eating and 2 foods that you do not enjoy eating yet
- Level 3: Choose 3 foods that you do not enjoy eating yet

2) Choose your taste profile.
   Here are some examples of different foods that pair well with whipped cream:

- Fruity:

   Strawberry, blueberry, oranges, slice of apple, raspberry

- Other:

   Chocolate, Graham crackers, cookies, granola, marshmellow

WHIPPED DRAWING

Put the whipped cream on a big plate or baking sheet. Make sure to spread the whipped cream using your hands.

Optional: You can also color the whipped cream with food coloring.

WHIPPED DRAWING

Choose a fruit of your choice, wash it, and cut it up if needed. Use the fruit to draw in the whipped cream. You can make different shapes, letters, or animals!

WHIPPED DRAWING

Optional step for more dazzle:
Want to decorate your work of art? Add some sprinkles, crushed graham crackers, nuts, or chocolate chips into the mix!

EXPERIMENT # 5
FUN COOKING

Description of activity:
Cook with your child

Goal:
This activity not only provides nutrient-dense treats, but it also allows your child to take the lead in the kitchen! Get messy and have fun! The most important part is the great bonding experience you will have with your child.

CHOCOLOCO CUPCAKES

*To make oat flour, blend oats until you reach a fine texture

Ingredients:

- ¾ cup of all-purpose flour
- ½ cup oat flour*
- ¼ cup cocoa powder
- 1 tsp baking soda
- 3 tsp flaxseeds, ground
- ¼ tsp salt
- 2 tbsp coconut oil, melted
- ¼ cup honey
- 1 tsp vanilla
- 1 egg
- 1 cup of zucchini, grated
- ½ ripe banana, mashed
- ½ cup almond milk, unsweetened
- ⅓ cup chocolate chips

Directions:

Step 1
Preheat the oven to 350 degrees F (175 degrees C). Line 9 muffin tins with parchment paper.

Step 2
Squeeze the excess water from the grated zucchini using paper towels.

Step 3
In a bowl, combine the all-purpose flour, oat flour, cocoa powder, baking soda, grounded flaxseeds and salt.

CHOCOLOCO CUPCAKES

Step 4

In a separate bowl, mix the coconut oil, honey, vanilla and egg. Use an electric mixer until well mixed (one consistency). Add the zucchini, banana, and almond milk. Mix well and fold in chocolate chips.

Step 5

Combine the dry and wet ingredients. Mix until one batter forms.

Step 6

Divide batter into prepared liners. Bake for 22 minutes or until a toothpick comes out clean. Let it cool.

Step 7

(Optional): Decorate with icing and/or fruits.

SUPERDUPER COOKIES

*To make oat flour, blend oats until you reach a fine texture

Ingredients:

- [ ] 1 cup of oat flour*
- [ ] 4 tbsp of brown sugar
- [ ] 1 tsp baking soda
- [ ] 3 tsp flaxseeds, ground
- [ ] ¼ tsp salt
- [ ] 1 tsp vanilla
- [ ] 2 tbsp coconut oil, melted
- [ ] 4 tbsp almond milk, unsweetened
- [ ] ¼ cup chocolate chips
- [ ] ⅓ cup of walnuts, chopped
- [ ] 3 tsp of all-purpose flour

Directions:

Step 1

Preheat the oven to 380 degrees F (195 degrees C). Line 9 muffin tins with parchment paper.

Step 2

In a bowl, combine and mix the oat flour, brown sugar, baking soda, ground flaxseeds and salt.

SUPERDUPER COOKIES

Step 3
Add in the vanilla, coconut oil, and almond milk. Stir well.

Step 4
Fold in the chocolate chips and chopped walnuts.

Step 5
If needed, add the all-purpose flour 1 tsp at a time until your batter is thick and hold its form when scooped.

Step 6
Scoop large spoonfuls of batter onto the prepared baking sheet.

Step 7
Bake for 9 minutes, and let it cool for 10 minutes (they will still cook as it cools down).

BUILD YOUR SMOOTHIE

Grab a blender and follow the steps below!

Step 1: Choose a liquid base

Water   Cow's Milk   Plant-Based Milk

Step 2: Add your protein

Regular Yogurt   Peanut Butter   Tofu

Greek Yogurt   Cashew

BUILD YOUR SMOOTHIE

Step 3: Add fruits and vegetables

Spinach + Strawberry + Banana

Carrot + Mango + Orange

Avocado + Blueberries + Banana

Step 4 (optional): Add a nutrition boost

Hemp Seeds   Chia Seeds   Flax Seeds

Draw or write your choices below!

+   +   +   = Your Smoothie!

Liquid base   Protein   Fruit & Vegetable   Nutrition Booster

BUILD YOUR SMOOTHIE

Sample Recipe

Ingredients:

- ☐ 1⁄2cup milk (or almond milk for dairy-free option)
- ☐ 1⁄2cup plain yogurt (or Greek yogurt)
- ☐ 1 ripe banana
- ☐ 1⁄2cup strawberries (fresh or frozen)
- ☐ 1⁄2cup blueberries (fresh or frozen)
- ☐ 1⁄2cup spinach leaves (fresh)
- ☐ 1 tbsp of chia seeds
- ☐ 1 tablespoon honey (optional, adjust to taste)
- ☐ Ice cubes (optional, for a colder smoothie)

Suggestions for Parents

- Choose ripe fruits for maximum sweetness. Alternatively, you can enhance the sweetness by adding honey or a sweetener of your choice to cater to your child's taste preferences.
- Customize the texture of your smoothie to suit your child's preferences. For those who enjoy thicker smoothies, reduce the amount of liquid and incorporate frozen fruits and vegetables. If your child prefers a more liquidy texture, add more liquid and omit frozen ingredients.
- If your child isn't keen on drinking smoothies, consider turning them into popsicles for a fun twist.
- Adjust the temperature of the smoothie to accommodate your child's preferences. Use room temperature liquids and fruits for kids who prefer warmer foods, while adding ice or frozen fruits/vegetables for those who enjoy colder treats.

CHECKING ON MY GOAL

Let's check on your goal (if you don't remember it, go back to page 19). Did you complete your goal? Circle your response.

I Did!

Not Yet!

My new goal is to:

(circle the action you want to do)

lick

chew and spit

chew and swallow

____

Write a food that you would like to try

so that I can grow strong and healthy.

CONGRATULATIONS!

The **ABC Yum Explorer** title goes to:

____

your name here

For being brave enough to explore
different foods throughout this book.